The Bears Who Went to the Seaside

Written and illustrated by
SUSANNA GRETZ

First published 1972 by Ernest Benn Limited, London. All rights reserved. This edition is published by Scholastic Book Services, a division of Scholastic Magazines, Inc., by arrangement with Follett Publishing Company, a division of Follett Corporation.
1st printing March 1975 .... Printed in the U.S.A.

SCHOLASTIC BOOK SERVICES
NEW YORK · TORONTO · LONDON · AUCKLAND · SYDNEY · TOKYO

Once on a hot summer afternoon
five bears set off for the beach.
William sat in the driver's seat.
Charles read the map;
Andrew climbed into the car,
wearing his new hat.
Robert handed the beach ball to John.
Fred, the dog, was panting to be off.

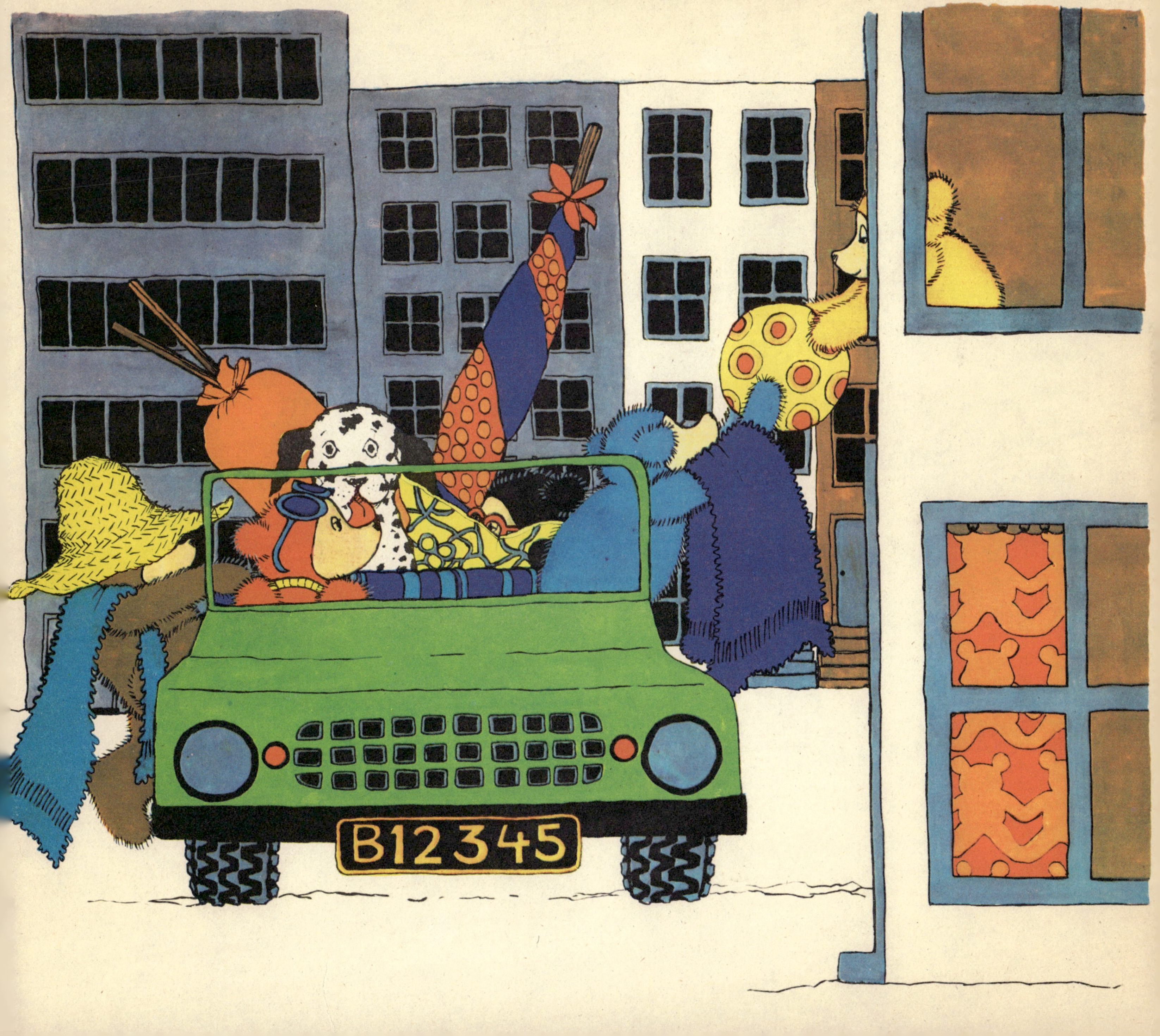
B12345

"Turn left for the beach," said Charles.
William turned left.
"Fred's ears are inside out," said Robert.
"It's the breeze," explained William.
Soon they came to the beach.

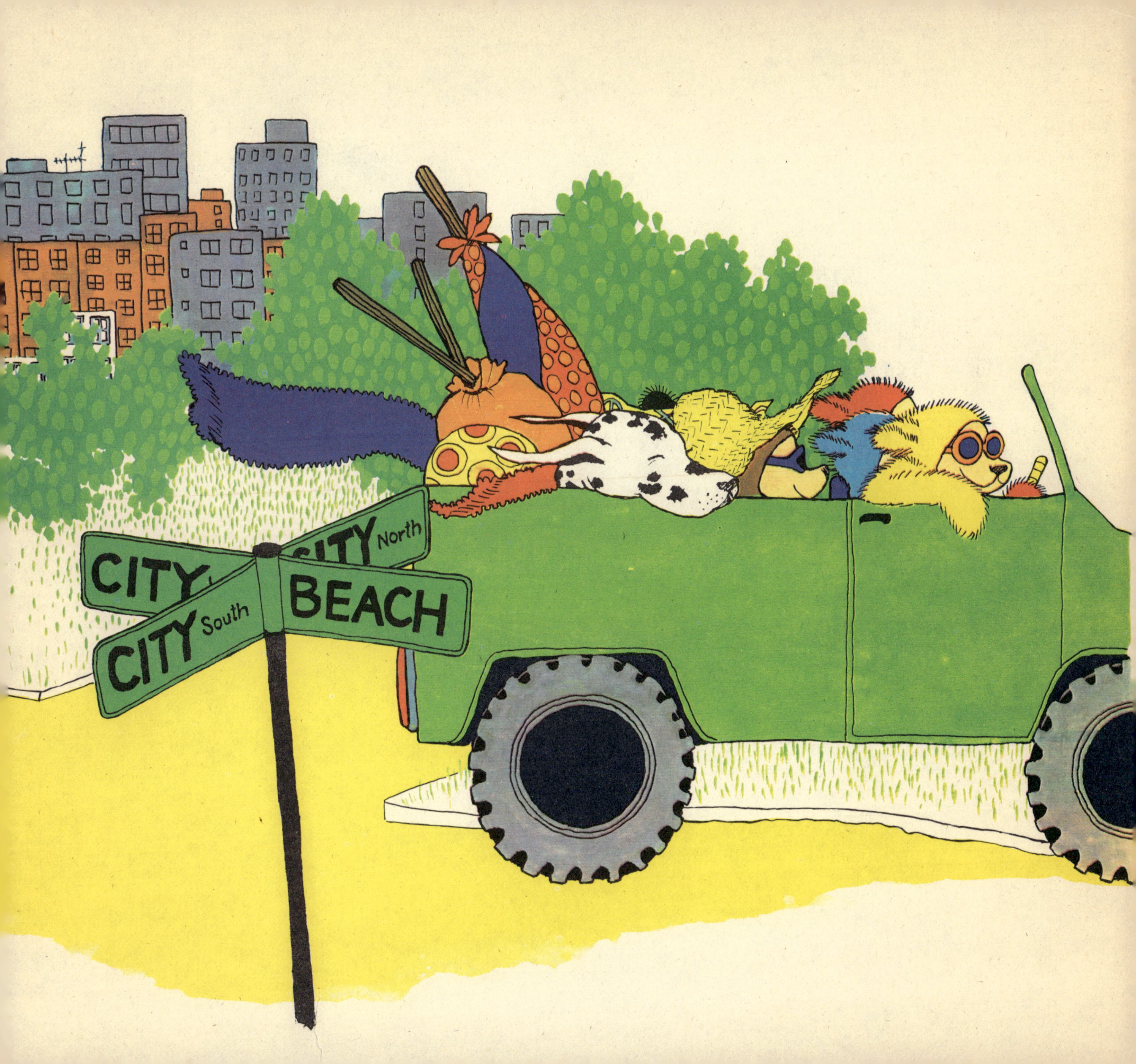
CITY
CITY North
CITY South
BEACH

"This is a good spot," said Charles,
but Robert had stepped on some tar.
"It's *not* a good spot," he said.
"Let's go this way," said Andrew.
"No—that way!" said John.
Fred didn't mind which way they went.

PARKING →

At last they found a good spot.
Then everyone was busy.
Robert, John and Andrew put up the tent.
William made certain that
all the food was there.
Charles tested the water.
Fred tested the water, too. Too cold!

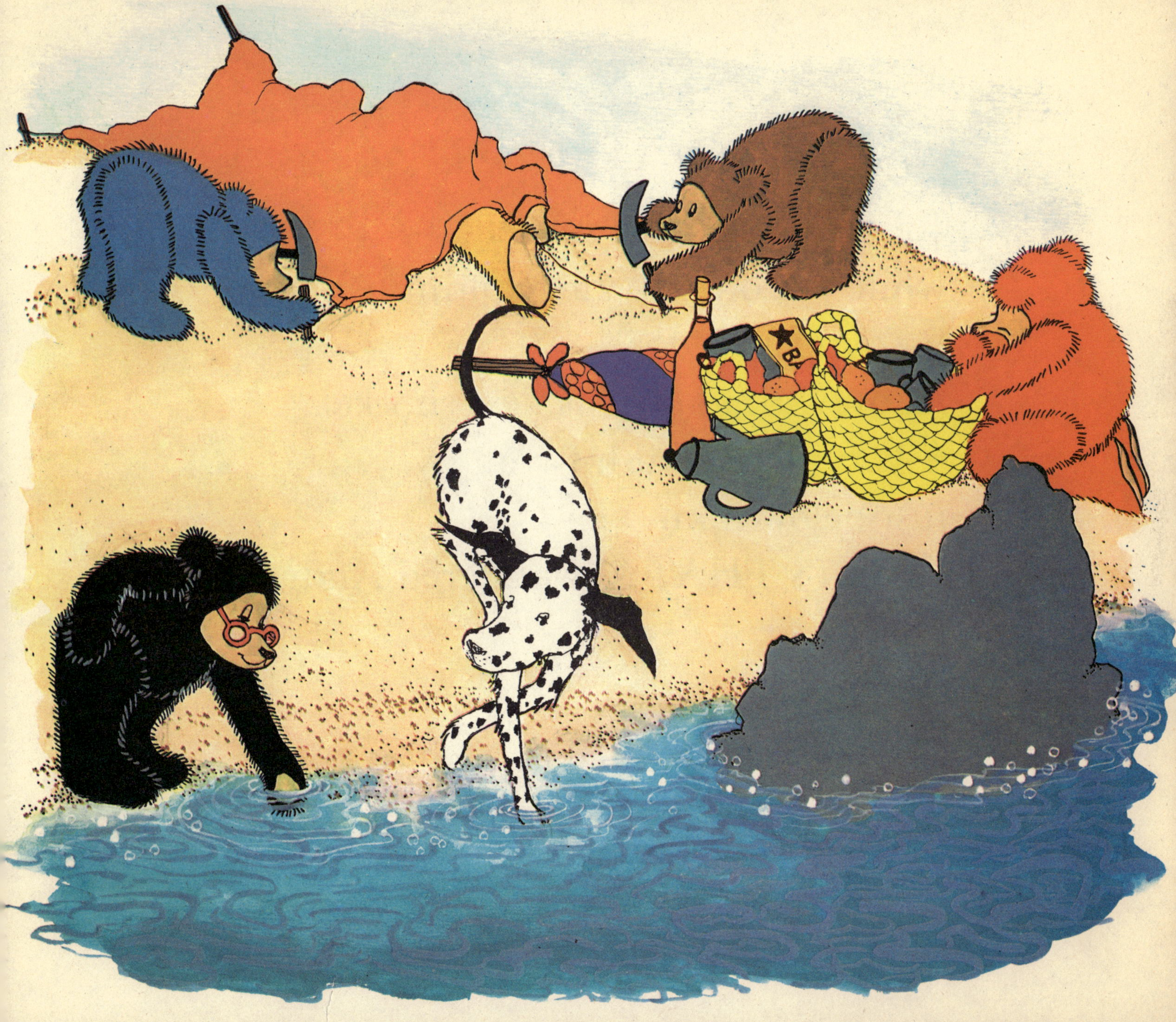

John watched the sunset,
while the other bears caught fish
for supper.
Andrew tried out his new snorkel.
A very strange fish swam by,
just below him.
"What's THAT?" wondered Andrew.

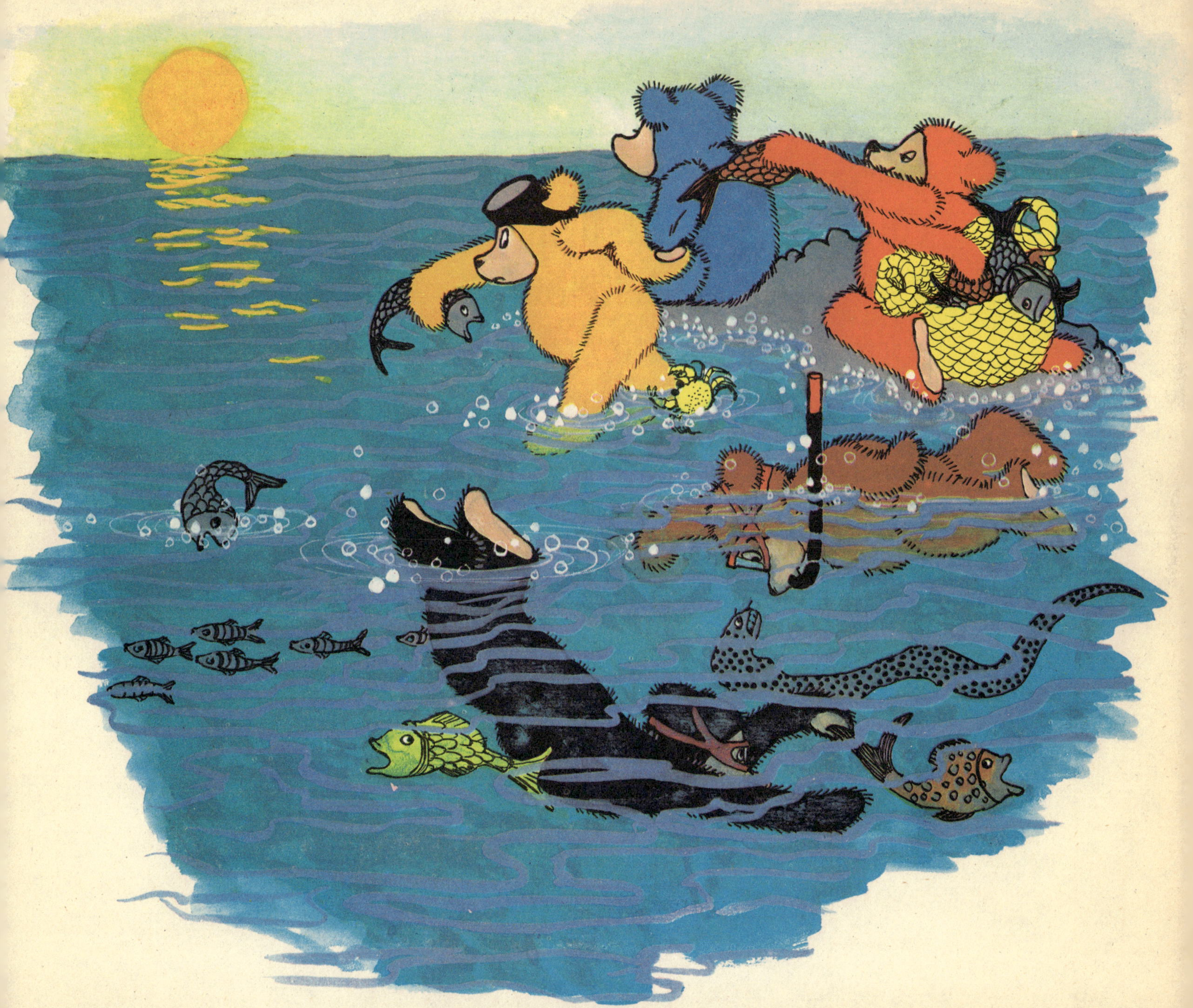

Charles fried the fish.
They were so delicious
that William ate *fifteen*.
"What's the matter with William?"
asked Andrew.
"I feel funny," answered William,
"*very* funny!"

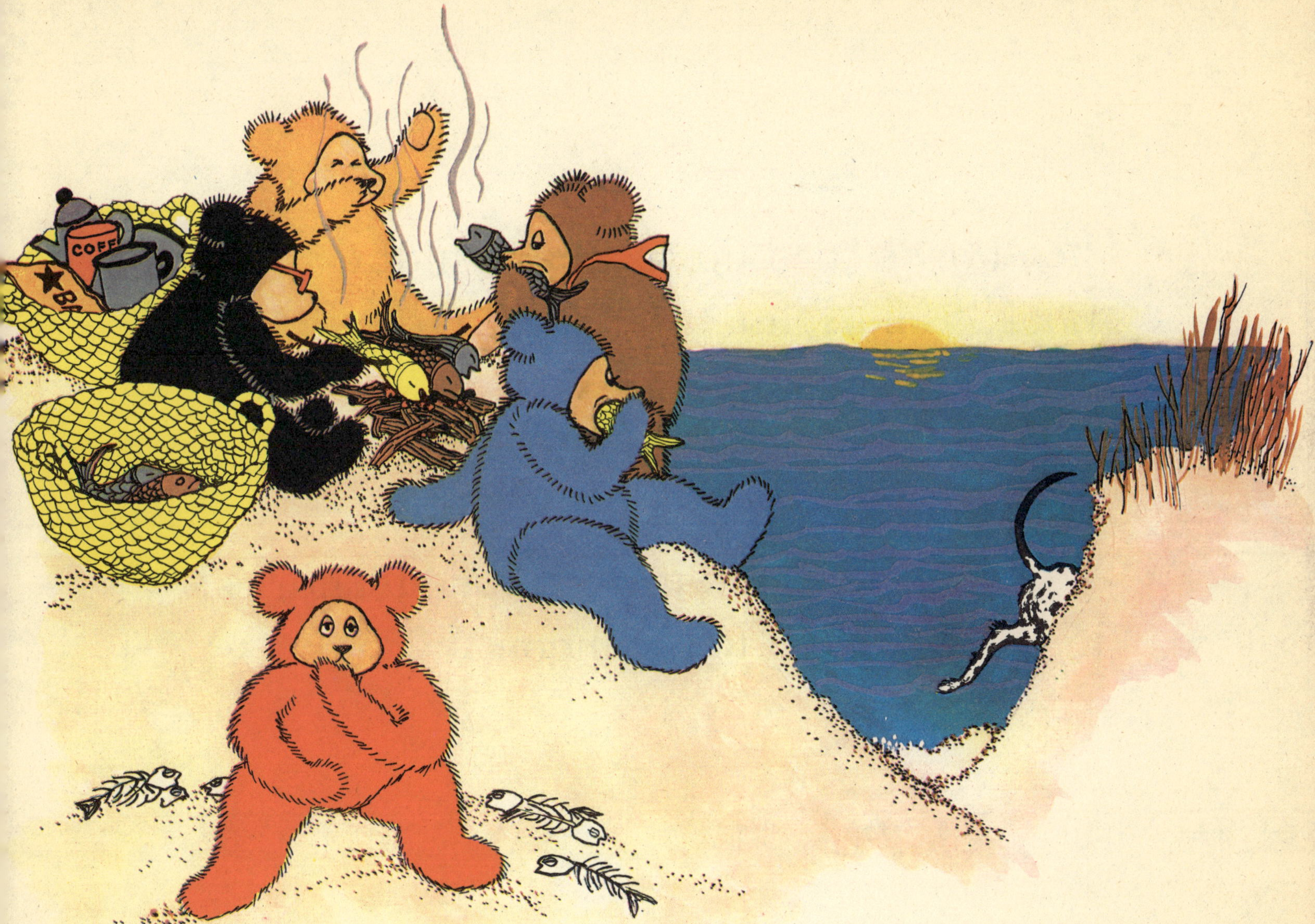

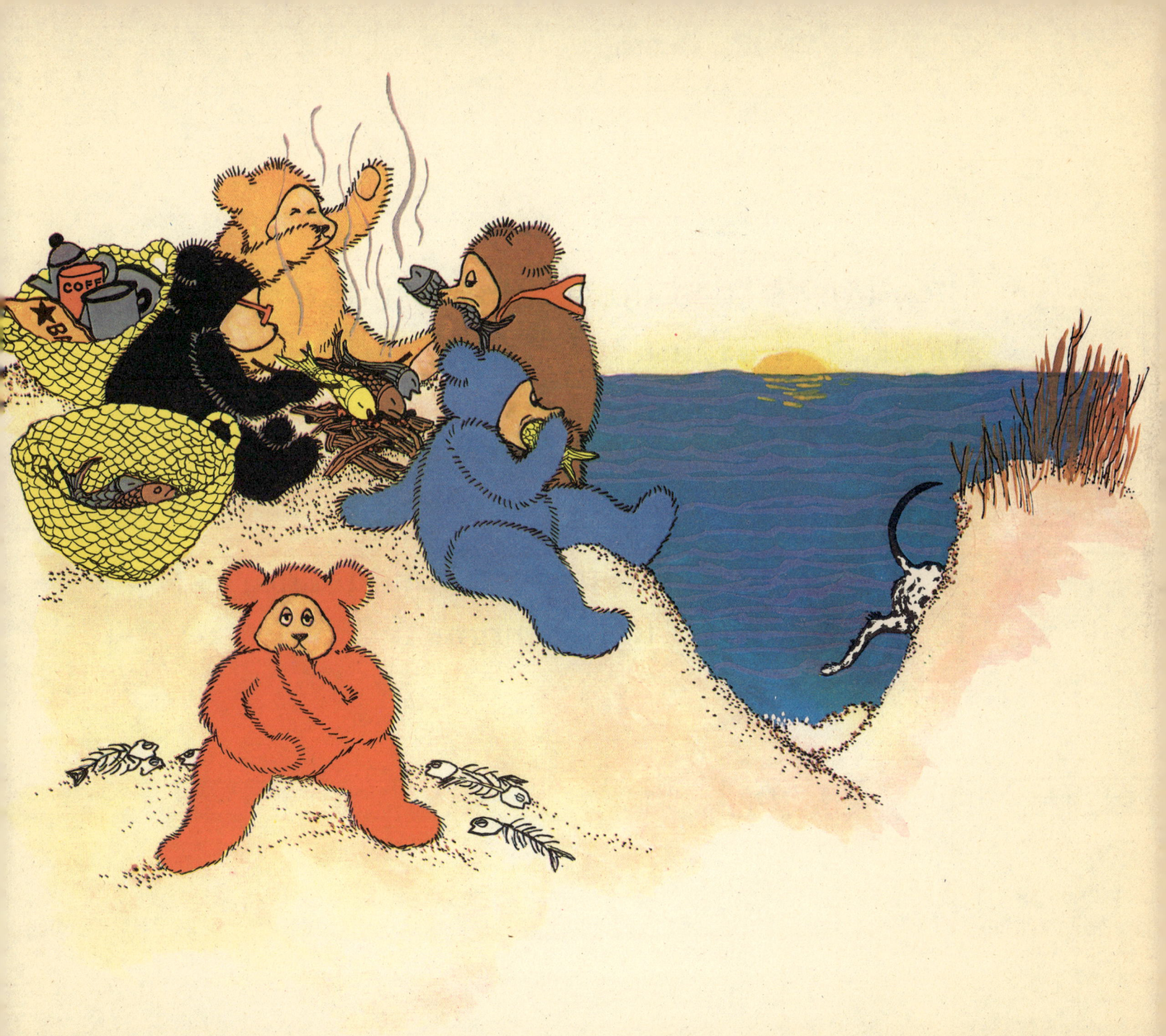

Then they settled down for the night.
"Look," said John, "that's the Great Bear,"
but nobody was interested.
"What's that howling noise?"
asked Andrew.
"What do you think it is?" replied Charles;
"it's Fred talking to the moon."

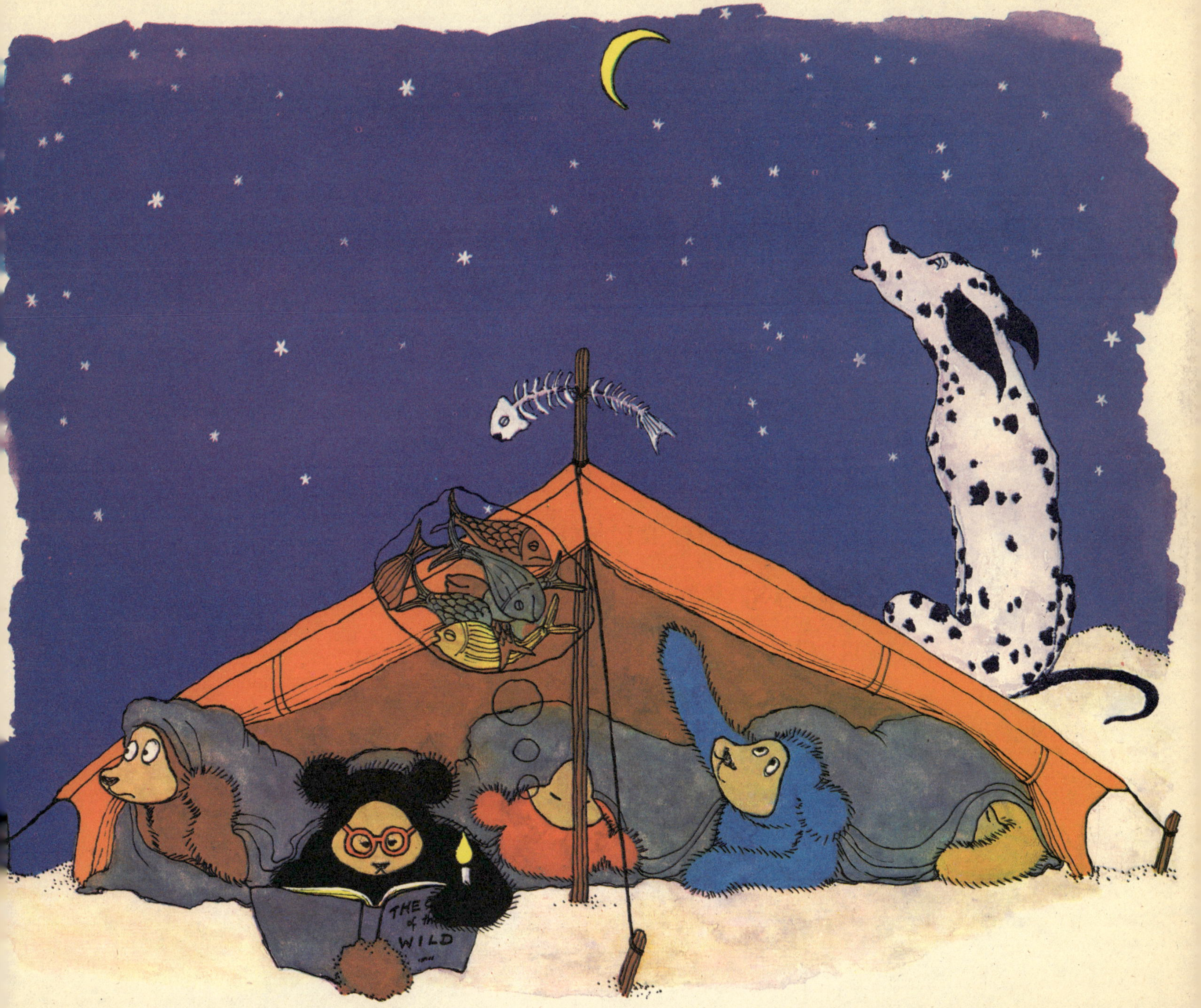
THE
WILD

Early the next morning John started
to build a sandcastle.
"It's time for an early morning dip,"
said Andrew.
Charles and Fred didn't want a dip
so early in the morning.
"It's much too early to get up,"
yawned Charles.

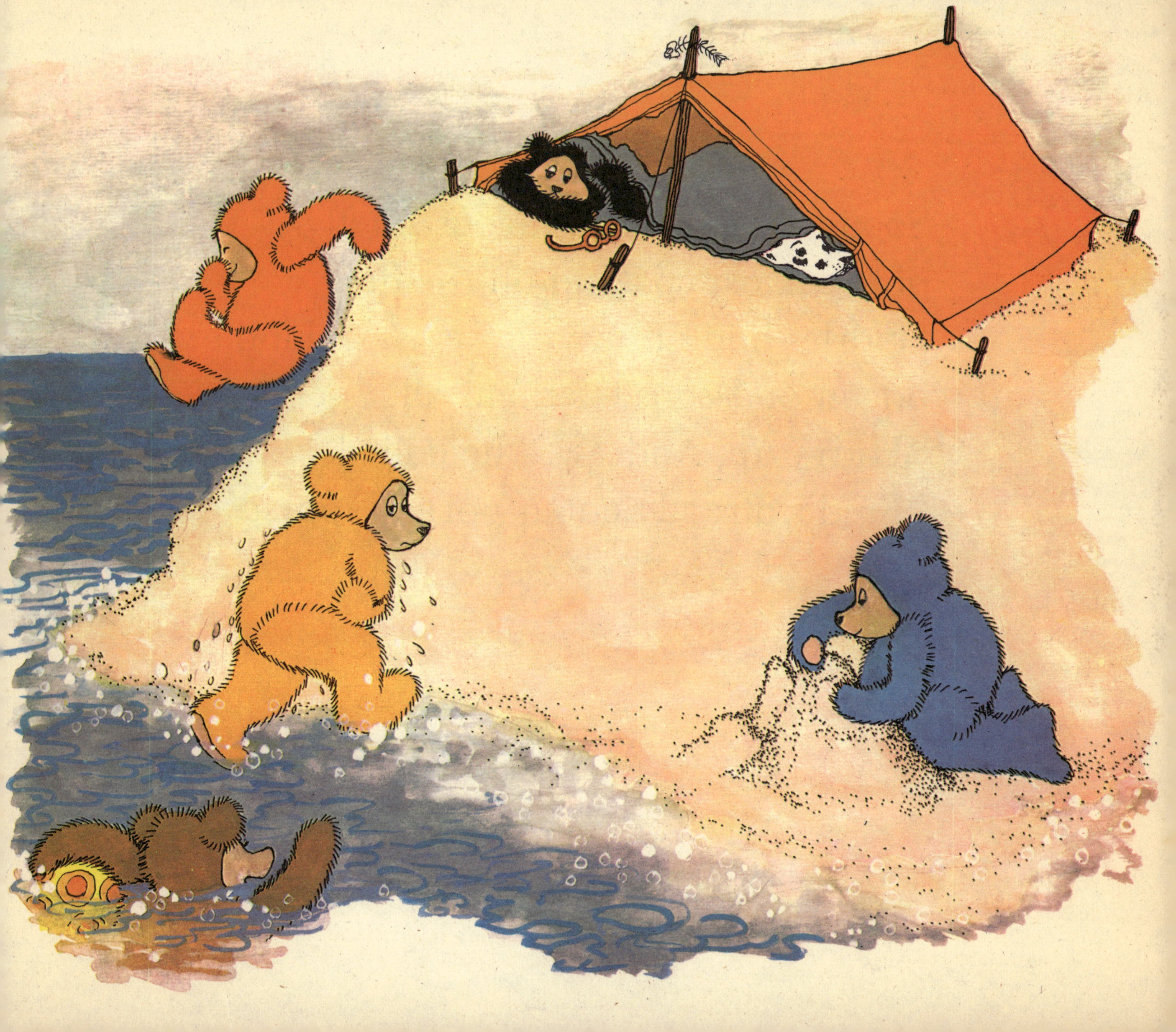

Soon there was a delicious smell
of breakfast cooking on the fire.
Charles had got up and was cooking
bacon and eggs for them all.
"Hurry up, Andrew," he called.
"Fred's already eaten part of yours."

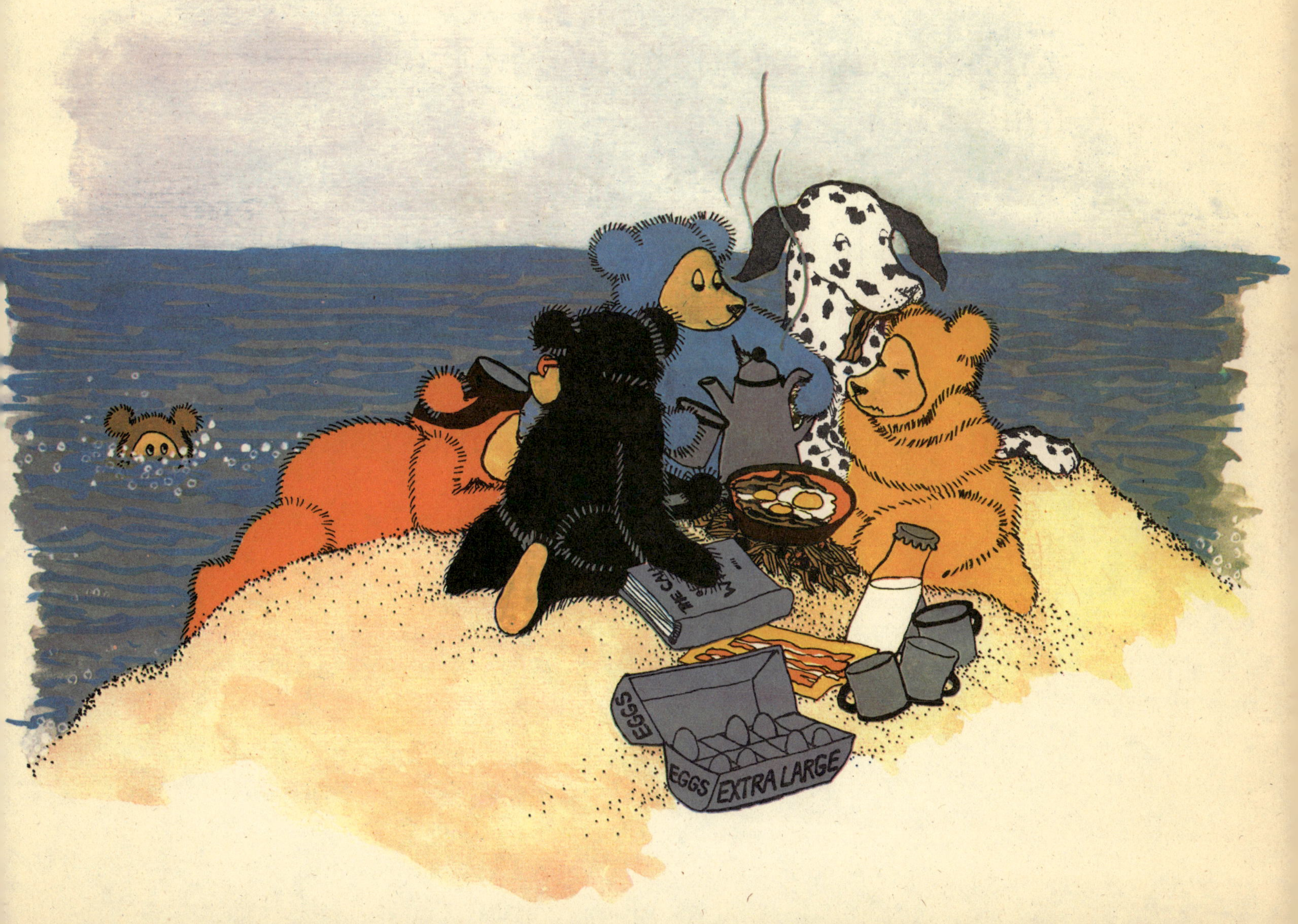
EGGS
EGGS EXTRA LARGE

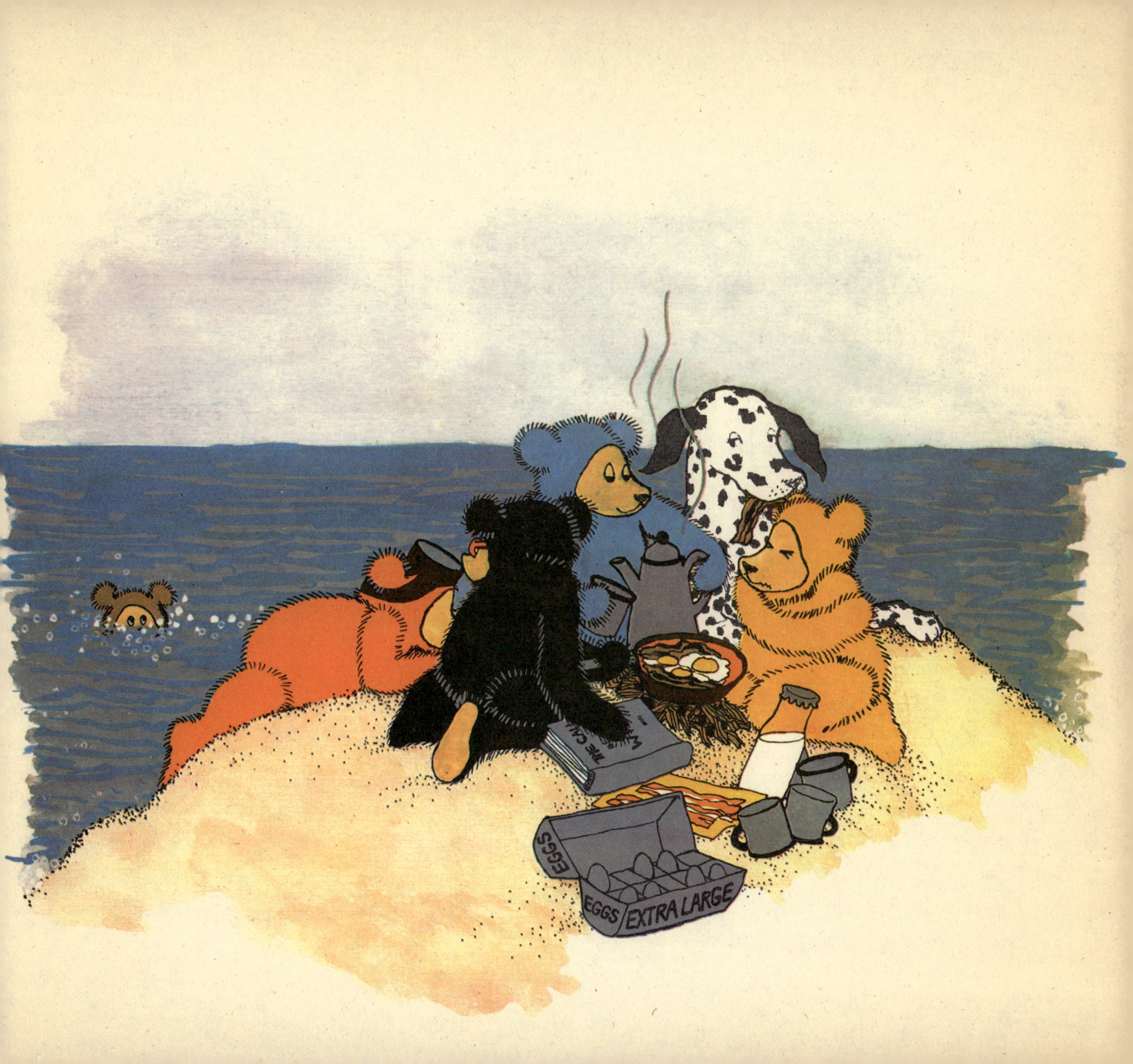

After breakfast Andrew and Robert
had a game of ball.
William stood between them trying
to catch the ball.
"Oops!" he said. "I don't seem to be able
to jump as high as I used to."
John was still building his sandcastle.

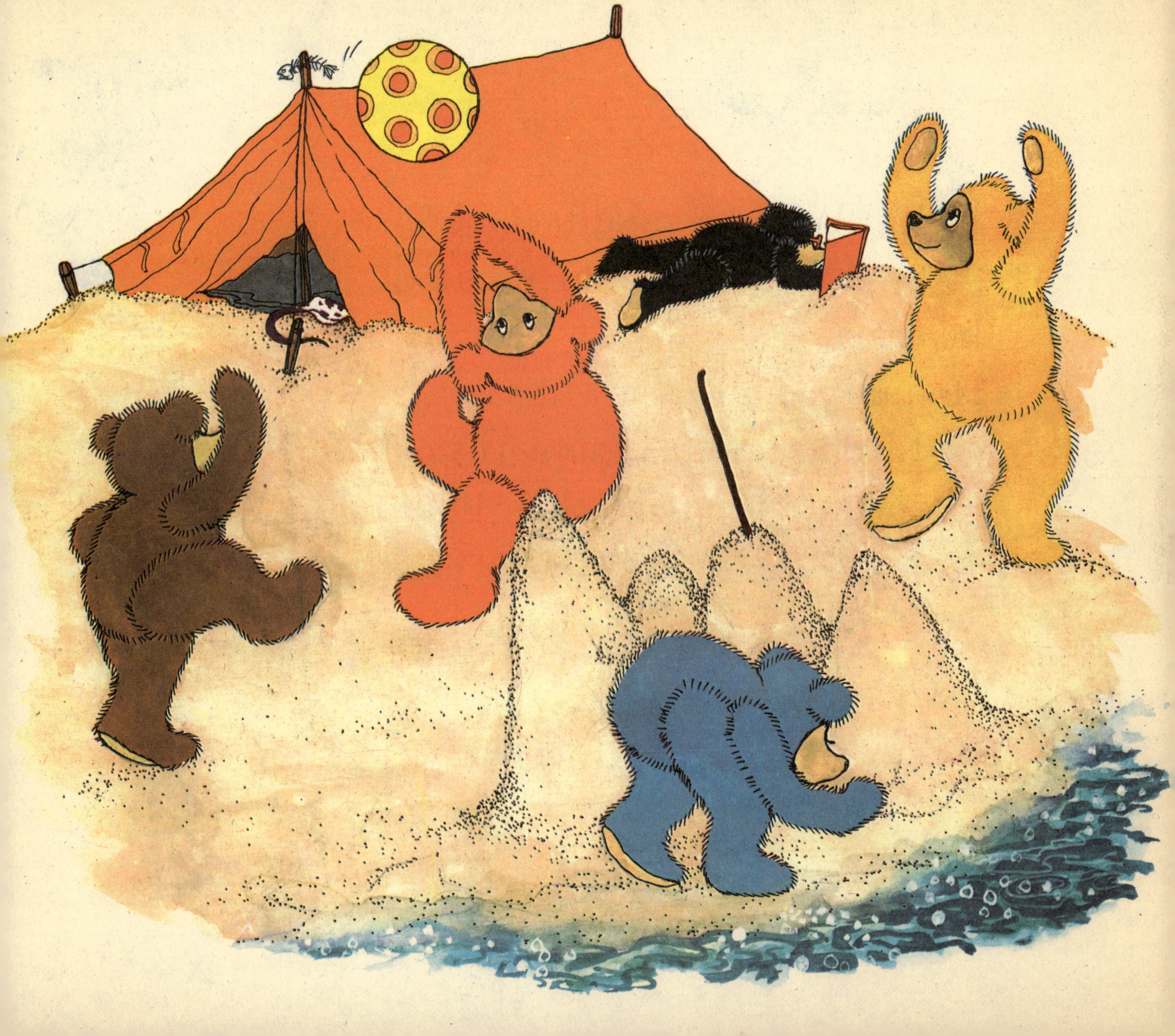

At last William caught the ball.
"Now I've got it, you try and get it back,"
he cried.
He jumped into the water,
and Robert and Andrew rushed after him.
"Look out for my castle," John told Fred.

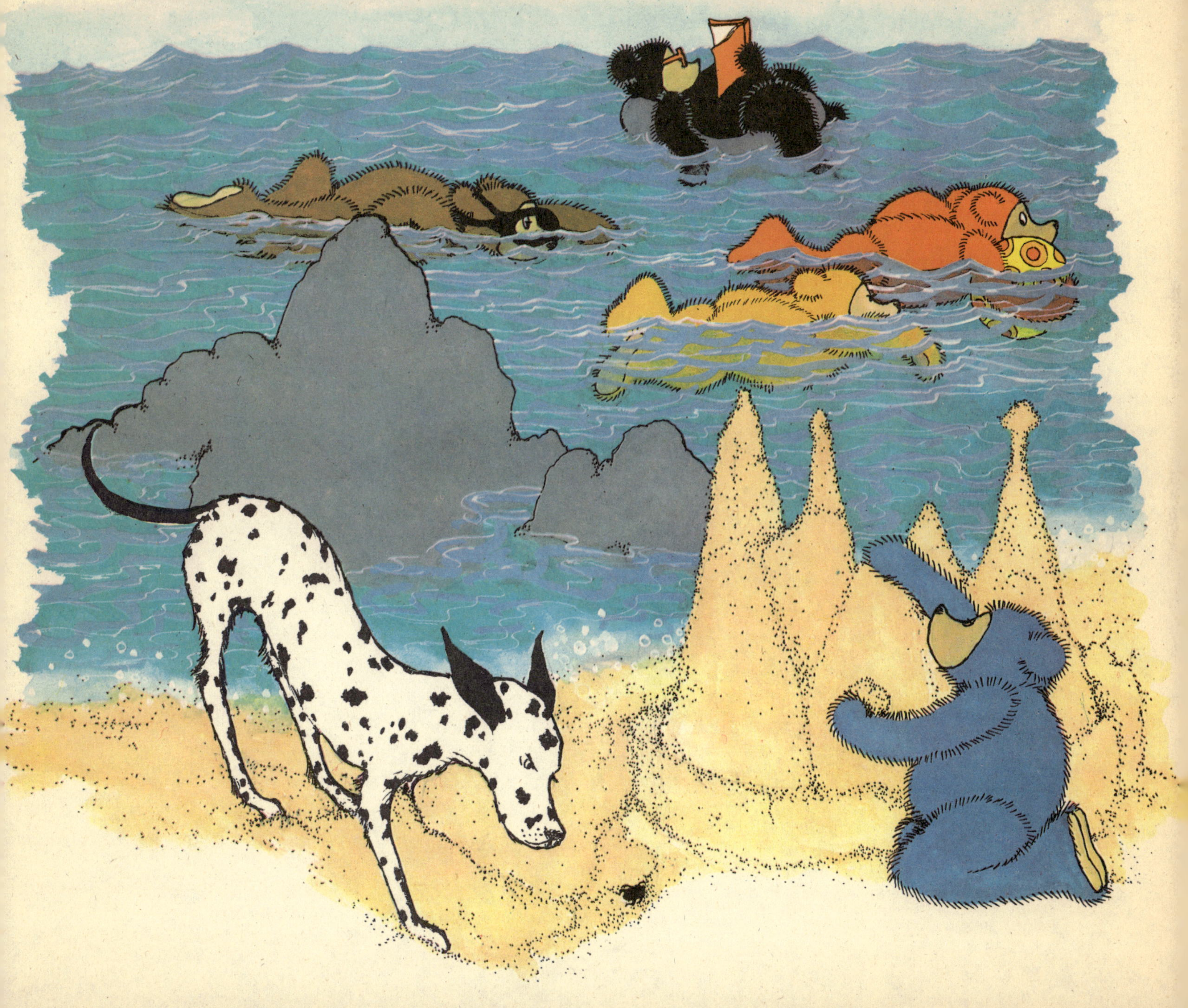

The sun became very hot.
"It's too hot even to read," said Charles.
Everyone lay down for a long sunbath—
that is, everyone except John.
He had to finish his sandcastle.

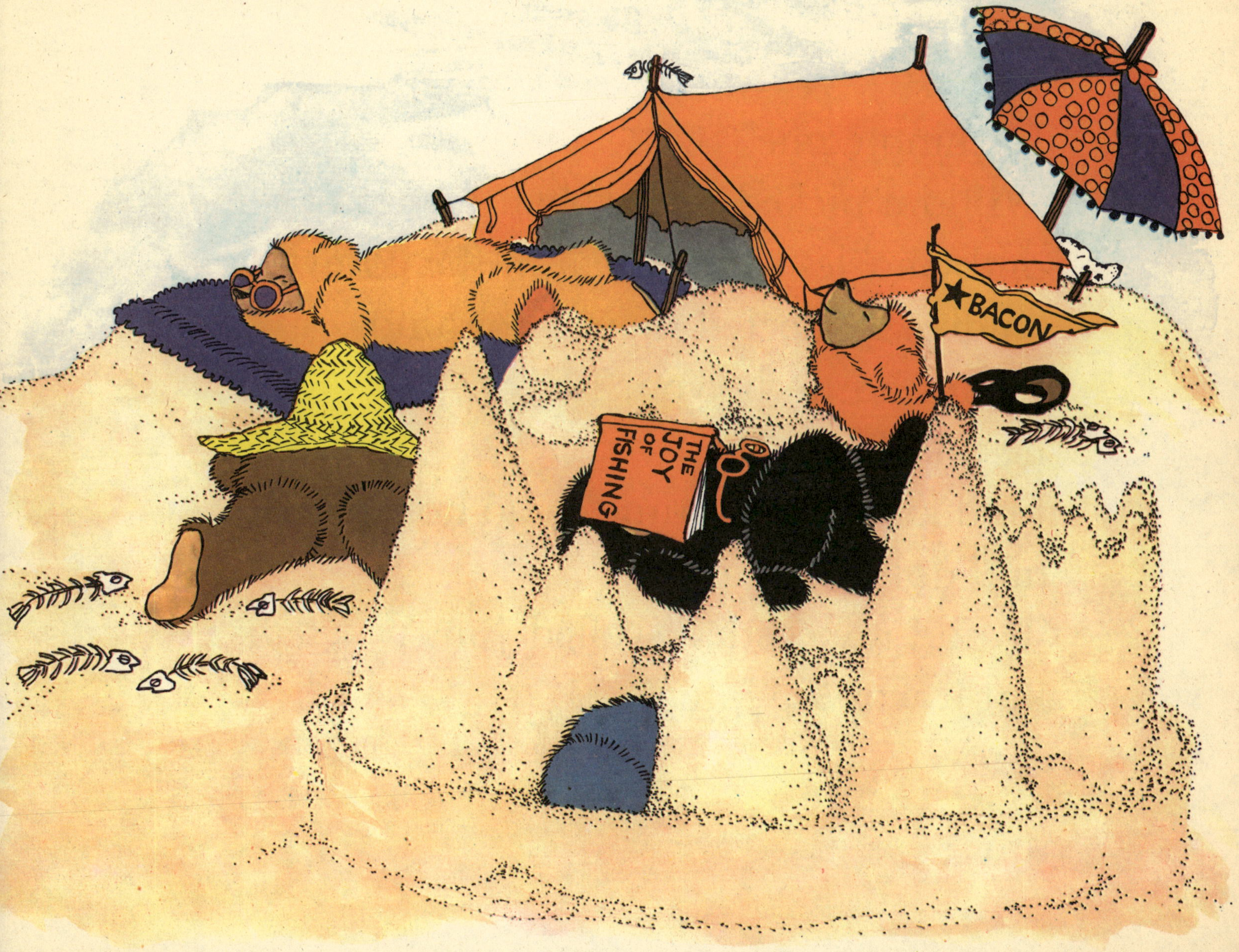
BACON
THE JOY OF FISHING

Evening came.
William picked up all their scraps of paper
and Charles burnt them in the campfire.
Andrew collected their belongings.
"That has to be your last dip,"
he told Robert.
Fred knew it was time to go home, too,
and got very excited.
"Mind my castle!" yelled John;
but it was too late.

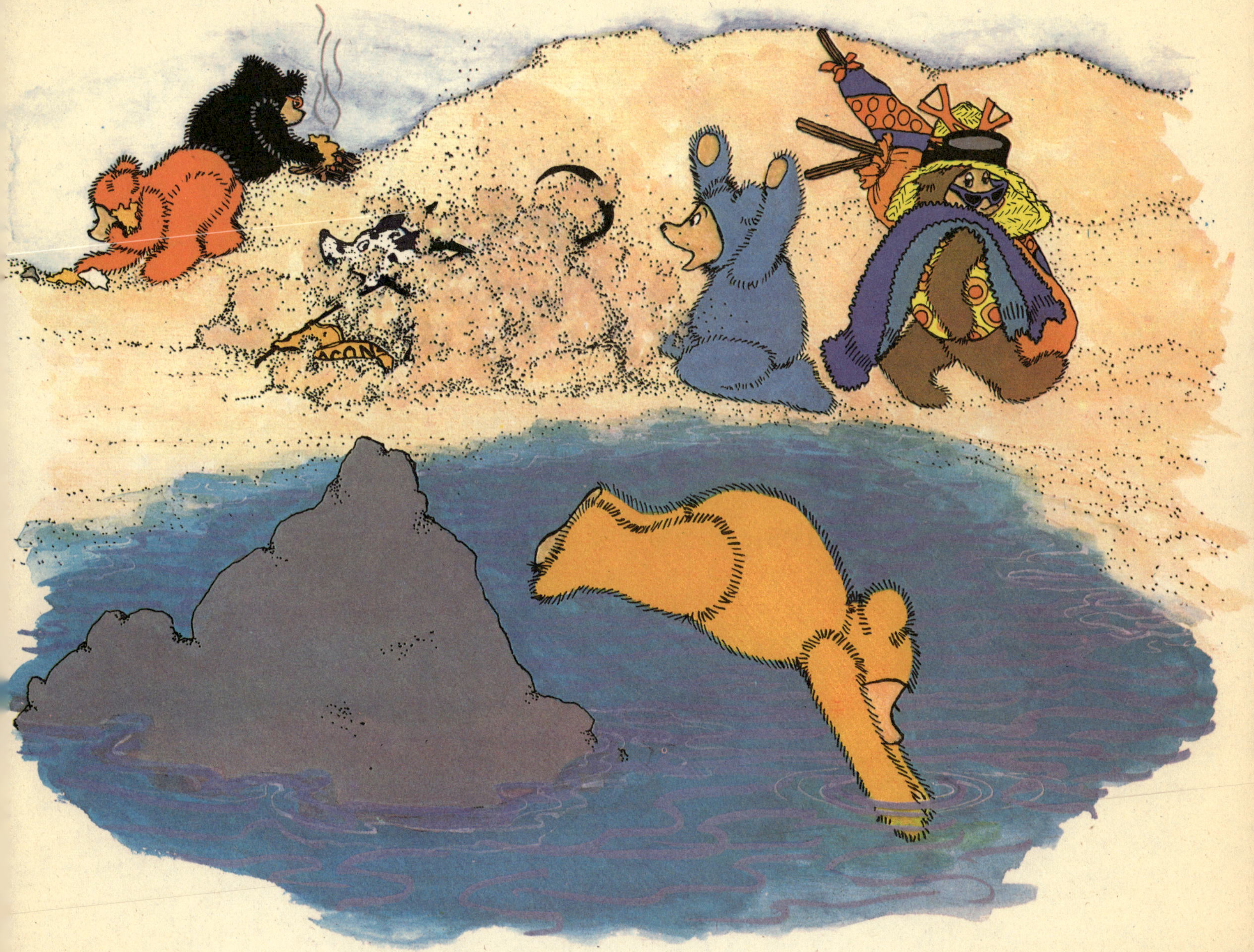

"My beautiful castle," said John
when they were all packed into
the car again.
"You can build a better one next time,"
said Charles.
"I've got a very interesting book
about castles."

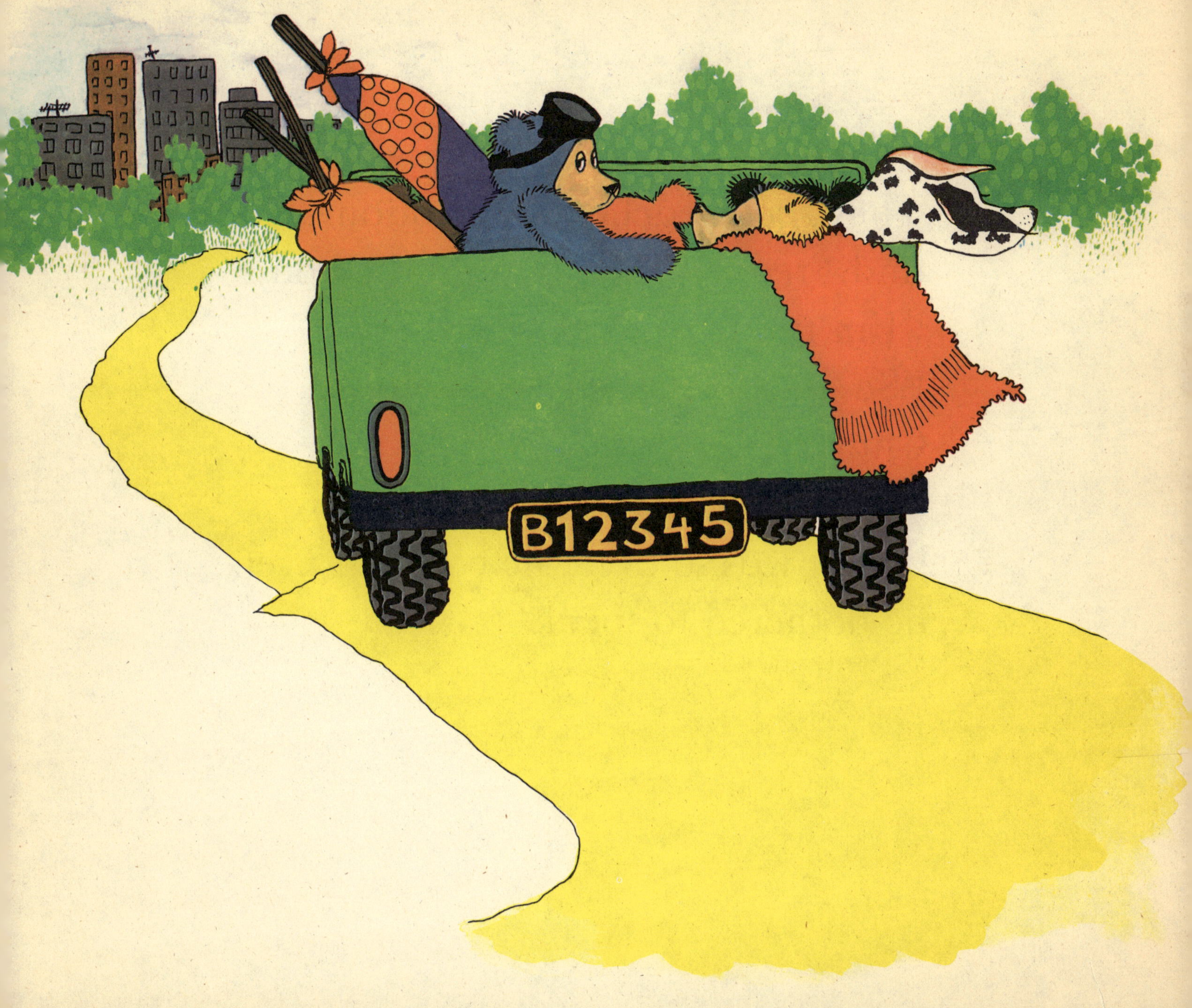
B12345

They soon reached home again,
and Fred led the way into the house.
"I'm tired," said William.
"So am I," agreed Andrew,
Charles and John.
So was Robert;
but he was so tired, he couldn't even
be bothered to speak.